TWISTED

HOUSE OF
A MILLION
ROOMS

Wil Mara

An imprint of Enslow Publishing

WEST **44** BOOKS™

THE VIDEOMANIAC   WHERE DID MY FAMILY GO?
HOUSE OF A MILLION ROOMS THE GIRL WHO GREW NASTY THINGS
THE TIME TRAP

Please visit our website, www.west44books.com. For a free color catal• of all our high-quality books, call toll free
1-800-542-2595 or fax 1-877-542-2596.

Cataloging-in-Publication Data

Names: Mara, Wil.
Title: House of a million rooms / Wil Mara.
Description: New York : West 44, 2019. | Series: Twisted
Identifiers: ISBN 9781538383636 (pbk.) | ISBN 9781538383582 (library bound) |
  ISBN 9781538383537 (ebook)
Subjects: LCSH: Haunted houses--Juvenile fiction. | Ghosts--Juvenile fiction.|
  Supernatural--Juvenile fiction.
Classification: LCC PZ7.M373 Ho 2019 | DDC [F]--dc23

Published in 2019 by
Enslow Publishing LLC
101 West 23rd Street, Suite #240
New York, NY 10011

Editor: Caitie McAneney
Designer: Rachel Rising

Photo Credits: Cover (people) Sean van Tonder/Shutterstock.com; Cover (house) Wit
tjaya/Shutterstock.com; Cover (background) STILLFX/Shutterstock.com.

Printed in the United States of America

CPSIA compliance information: Batch #CS18W44: For further information contact
Enslow Publishing LLC, New York, New York at 1-800-542-2595.

TWISTED

*For McKinli and Genevieve, who can light up my
day no matter how hard the rain.*

"Wow," Ryan whispered, "it's really there."

"I . . . I can't believe it," Samantha added.

"It's *so* cool," Josh said excitedly.

They stood along the edge of the forest. There was a long, open field in front of them. And in the middle of the field was a house. It was very old and very big. There was no paint on the outside. Just bare wood that had turned gray from years in the sun. Other than that, it looked to be in good shape. An old house, but a *strong* house.

They couldn't take their eyes off it. They just stood there getting soaked as the rain drove through the trees. It sounded like popcorn in the microwave.

"It's really been here all this time?" Samantha asked. Her long, dark hair was stuck to the sides of her face.

Ryan shrugged. He was the smallest of the three. He was also the only one who wore glasses. "I guess so," he said. "The note was from 1953."

Ryan found the note in an old book. He had been in the school library earlier that day. He was working on a report about colonial America. The library had six different books on the subject. Most of them were pretty new. One, however, looked like it was about to fall apart. Ryan loved books. Sure, the Internet was great. But there was nothing like a real book.

He took the old one off the shelf. The first thing he did was open it up and smell it. *Old books have the greatest smell in the world*, he thought. Then he started going through the pages. The pictures were all black and white. And they were drawings, not photographs. Ryan didn't think a book this old could help with the report. But he liked looking through it anyway.

Somewhere around the middle, he found a folded sheet of paper. It was caught between two pages. When he unfolded it, he saw writing from top to bottom. The ink wasn't black anymore. It had turned brown over time. Then he noticed the date at the top—June 7, 1953. *Wow*, he thought. *It's been here THAT long . . .*

There were two different types of handwriting. He read the first few lines—

Are you going to Alan's party on Saturday?
> I'm not sure. My mom and dad probably won't let me. Are you?

Yeah.
> It sounds like it'll be swell

It will be! You have to go!

This was some kind of a secret note, he

realized. Someone left it in a book. Then another person found it and wrote a reply. It went back and forth like that until whenever. *Today we just send text messages*, Ryan thought. But they didn't have cell phones in 1953.

He was pretty sure it was between a boy and a girl. The boy really wanted the girl to go to this party. He kept asking, and she kept giving reasons why she couldn't. *Bo-ring!* Ryan thought.

Then he turned the note over. There was more writing on the other side. At first it was just the same stuff. Then it wasn't so boring after all. In fact, it was anything *but—*

Greg and I are going to check out that old house.
    What old house?
The one out on the west side of town. Through the woods.
    You know you can't do that!
Why not?

Carl, that place is bad news! And if you get caught, you'll get in SO much trouble!

I hear it's haunted! Who wouldn't want to check out a house that's haunted? It'll be a blast!

It doesn't matter! You know no one is allowed to go near it! NOBODY!

That's what my mom said when I asked her about it.

My parents have told me over and over never to go near it! They bug me about it at least once a year! One time I asked them why, and they grounded me for a week!

My mom told me never to ask about it again. Boy, was she mad!

Carl, PLEASE promise me you won't go near it! PLEASE???

Will you go to Alan's with me on Saturday?

Yes, yes, I'll figure something out. But please promise me!

Okay, I promise.

Ryan showed Josh the note. Then Josh

showed Samantha. A few hours later, here they were.

"Have you ever even *heard* anyone talk about it?" Ryan asked.

Samantha shook her head. "Not me."

"I haven't either," Josh said. He was tall for his age and very athletic. He had brown hair that was thick up top but short around the sides. "But I've heard stories about things that have happened in this area."

"I heard the ground around here has poison in it or something," Samantha said.

"Right," Josh went on. "Some kind of government testing, years and years ago."

"Yeah."

"Can you imagine it?" Josh wondered. "Government testing here in the little town of Fairmont."

Ryan was nodding. "I heard the same thing. But . . ." He took out his iPhone and held it up.

He used his other hand to cover it from the rain. "I've got an app on here that detects dangerous radiation. Y'know—electromagnetic waves."

Josh rolled his eyes and smiled. "Of course you do."

Ryan looked closely at the screen. "And there doesn't seem to be any. Not even a tiny bit."

Josh turned back to the house and put his hands on his hips. The rain had matted his brown hair flat to his head.

"So what's the big deal, then?"

"No idea."

"And the fence, too," Josh went on. "With all those signs."

When they were walking through the woods to get there, they came to a fence. It was the metal kind with all the diamond-shaped holes. And there were signs on it that said **DANGER—DO NOT ENTER**. Josh had to bend the fence up at the bottom so they could crawl through.

"I'll bet there's more to this," he said. "We should check it out."

At that moment, a roll of thunder boomed in the distance. Then came a flash of lightning.

"Not now," Samantha said. "The storm's getting worse."

"We should get out of here," Ryan added. "Being near trees when there's lightning is a really bad idea."

Josh didn't seem to hear them. He was still staring at the house.

"I wonder what's in there . . ." he said finally. It sounded like he was talking mostly to himself.

Lightning cracked again. This time it was very close.

"Josh, come on," Samantha said, grabbing his hand.

"Huh?" He seemed like he'd been in a trance. "Oh, yeah. Okay. But I'm coming back."

"That's probably a bad idea," Samantha

replied. "But either way—not today. Let's go."

"Before the lightning fries us," Ryan said. "Like three eggs."

"Okay, okay," Josh told them. He kept looking back, though. It was as if the house held some kind of power over him.

After they were gone, lightning struck one more time. It hit so close that the whole house seemed to light up. And at that moment, a shape appeared in one of the upstairs windows.

The shape of a person.

An hour later, Josh Harper was sitting at his parents' dinner table. His mom had made a nice meatloaf. Meatloaf was one of his favorites. She also made the buttered noodles that he loved.

"Everyone dig in!" she said as she sat down. She had that little smile on her face. It was the smile she *always* had, no matter what mood she was really in. Josh thought she was the greatest mom in the world.

"A little dry," his dad grumbled. Josh loved him, too. But they didn't get along as well as Josh would've liked.

Josh looked to his mom. Her smile seemed to fade for just a moment. It was like a candle that was flickering and about to go out. Then it came back when she said, "How was your day, guys?"

"I got another A in math," Ethan piped up. He was wearing a big smile, too. But it wasn't kind like his mom's. *It's the smug smile of a snotty little brat*, Josh thought.

Their dad finally looked up from his plate. "You did? Atta boy! I'm proud of you!"

Of course he's proud, Josh thought. *Dad's an accountant. He works all day with numbers. Numbers are his life.*

"Fourth A in a row," Ethan added. Because, of course, he was keeping count.

"You're the *man!*" his dad said, pointing at him. Josh felt like he wasn't even in the room. But that feeling wouldn't last long.

Ethan turned to him. That snotty smile was still in place. "When was the last time *you* got an A in math, Joshie?"

Josh could feel his cheeks turning red. And

he knew everyone else could see it, too. Everyone except his dad, that is. He had already gone back to his meatloaf. His *dry* meatloaf.

"I don't know," Josh said. He kept his voice calm. He knew it would drive Ethan crazy. Ethan was trying to get under his skin. But if Josh didn't show any anger, Ethan would lose.

Then Josh said, "It's probably been as long as the last time you got an A in English."

Ethan's smile fell. It looked like it had been held up by wires that had suddenly been cut.

"Josh, that's enough," his dad said quietly.

Josh looked at him in shock. He was unable to believe what he'd just heard. *You want ME to leave him alone? How about telling HIM the same thing? And HE STARTED IT!*

But Josh knew that wouldn't happen. Ethan could do no wrong in their dad's eyes. He was the perfect child.

When Josh turned back, he saw that Ethan

was smiling again. Josh would've done anything to wipe that smile off his face. *Like smack it off,* Josh thought.

They ate in silence for a few minutes. Then Josh said, "Hey, something really interesting happened today."

"What's that?" his mom asked. She looked happy to be talking about something else now.

"Well, Ryan found this old note between the pages of a library book."

"Oh?"

"Yeah, it was really cool. From 1953."

His mom's eyes widened. "Really?" She touched her husband's hand. "Jack, did you hear that?"

He nodded but never looked up from his food. "Yeah."

"What did it say?" she asked.

"Well, it was like two people talking. One wrote something, then the other wrote something back. I think it was a boy and a girl. At first they were talking about going to this party."

His mom smiled while she cut off another piece of meatloaf. "As young boys and girls will do," she said.

"Right. But then they talked about something else. This old house on the other side of Fairmont. You have to walk through the woods to get there, and—"

Josh stopped because everyone else did, too. His dad was just about to take a sip of milk from his glass. He froze with the glass halfway up. His mom had that last piece of meatloaf almost to her mouth. She froze that way, too. And Ethan froze simply because his parents froze. They all looked like people in a photograph.

Finally, his dad turned to him. He looked more interested in Josh than he ever had before.

"Where did you say it was?"

"On the far side of town," Josh said. Then

he pointed over his back, as if that actually helped. "I think it's west from here."

His dad and mom looked at each other. Words seemed to flow silently between them. Josh didn't know what those words were. But he knew one thing for certain. *They know which house I'm talking about.*

"Did you . . . did you *go up* to the house?" his mom asked. There was real fear in her voice. There was quite a bit in her eyes, too.

"No," Josh replied. "The storm from before was getting bad. Lightning and everything. So we were thinking—"

"No, Josh. Let me tell you what you're thinking," his dad said, cutting him off. He set his glass back down. Then he used his finger to point again, just like he had with Ethan. But there was no happiness in his face this time. In fact, he looked more than just angry. He looked like he could explode at any minute.

"You're thinking," he went on, "that you will never go near that house again. *That's* what you're thinking. Do you understand me?"

"Dad—"

"No, you listen close. You will *never* go near it again. You won't go near it. You won't talk about it. You won't think about it. You won't *anything* it. You got that?"

Josh didn't know what to say. He looked to his mom. The fear was still swimming in her eyes. Then he turned to Ethan. Josh thought he'd be all happy. He was always happy when Josh got in trouble. But Ethan looked frightened, too. Very frightened.

Then Josh felt something touch his shoulder. He looked back and saw that his dad had poked him. *With his finger . . . he actually reached over and poked me with it!* His dad could be pretty mean when he wanted to be. But he *never* touched either of his boys.

"Hey," his dad said. "Are you hearing me?"

"Yes."

Now the finger was pointing at him again. It looked like his dad was tapping something in the air.

"If you go to that house again and I find out . . . you'll be one sorry kid. I promise you that. Am I completely clear?"

"Yes, completely."

His dad kept watching him for another few seconds. They were the longest seconds of Josh's life. Then, finally, his dad got out of his chair and left the room. There was still plenty of food on his plate. But that didn't matter.

Dinner was over.

"My parents freaked, too," Ryan said.

The three of them were sitting in the bleachers by the school's baseball field. There was no game or practice this afternoon, so they were alone. And everything around them was still soaked from yesterday's storm.

"My dad's eyes popped open real wide," Ryan went on. "It looked like his eyeballs might fall out. Then he sent me to my room! I can't remember the last time that happened!"

"I can't believe *my* parents got upset," Samantha told them. "They never get worked up about anything!"

"What did they say about the house?" Ryan

asked her.

"They were like, 'We don't want you going there!'" She said this in a low voice, trying to sound like her dad. "'Please, Samantha, don't ever go there again!'"

"But they didn't tell you anything *about* the house?"

"Not a thing. I asked, but they wouldn't tell me anything."

Ryan shook his head. "It's so weird. We've lived on the same street all our lives. And I don't think I've ever heard your dad get upset. Not even once."

"He doesn't," Samantha said. "That was the freaky part. You know my parents. They're not very strict. They don't ever yell. They were like different people last night."

Josh hadn't spoken a word since they sat down. He was just staring into space.

Finally, he said, "There's something there.

Something in that house they don't want us to see."

"I can't imagine what," Ryan said. "It looked like an old house to me, that's it."

"Then why the fence?" Josh asked. "And all those warning signs? And why is it so far from everything else? We probably walked a half mile just to get to it."

"At least," Samantha said.

Josh turned to look at them. "And no one wants to *talk* about it! That's the part I don't get. Why? Why won't anyone even *talk* about it?"

Ryan shrugged. "No idea."

Josh smiled. It wasn't a happy smile or a funny smile. There was something else behind it.

"Then we should go find out," he told them. "We should go there. Go right up the steps and open the front door!"

Samantha looked fairly unhappy with this idea. Ryan, on the other hand, looked terrified.

"Are you crazy? You heard what our parents said!"

Josh was nodding. "Of course I heard them. But it's not going to stop me."

"Josh," Ryan pleaded. "Come on . . ."

"You're one of the smartest kids in school," Josh said to him. "You're going to tell me you're not curious? With that big brain of yours? You don't want to know what the big secret is?"

"Well, sure," Ryan replied. "I mean, part of me does. But I don't want to, um . . ."

"What?" Josh asked. "Get in *trouble*?"

"Well, yeah."

Josh shook his head. "You're such a chicken."

"I am not!"

"Yes you are. You're so worried about what everyone else thinks. You never do anything wrong."

"That's not true and you know it!" Ryan

barked. He was about a foot shorter than Josh. But he still looked like he'd fight him at that moment. "You're just mad at your dad! That's why you want to do this!"

Josh turned quickly to Ryan. "And you're just scared! That's why you *don't* want to do it!"

Samantha put her hands up. "Okay, okay. Both of you just calm down. Now, I think I know how we can do this without getting *anyone* into trouble."

"How's that?"

"The library."

Josh looked confused. "What?!"

"We can go to the library," she said. "It's got the big section on—"

"—town history!" Ryan finished for her. "That's a great idea!"

Samantha smiled. "I thought you'd like it."

"What about, like, Google? Or some other place online?" Josh asked.

Ryan shook his head. "I already looked. I couldn't find anything. And besides, this is *local* history. Samantha's right—the library's the place."

"Some of those books are really old," Josh said.

"Yeah—maybe as old as the house itself," Ryan told him. "I'm guessing it was built about eighty or ninety years ago. That's based on the general construction and design."

Josh reached over and messed up his hair. "Like I said—*smart.*"

Samantha smiled and got up. "Okay, children. Let's go check it out."

The school library was open for two hours after classes ended every day. Many students went there to do their homework before going home. Aside from all the books, there were plenty of computers and lots of sunlight. Ms. Krauze, the head librarian, made sure everything was always kept neat and orderly. Everyone called her "Ms. K."

"Here's the section," Samantha said, taking them down a short flight of stairs. One particular shelf had a little sign that said **LOCAL HISTORY.** There were about thirty books in total. Some looked to be very old, others fairly new. One title was *Fairmont in the 19th Century*. Another was *A Brief History of Fairmont*. A third was *Fairmont, Past and Present*.

"Which one?" Josh wondered.

But Ryan had already started pulling them down. "All of them, *duh* . . ."

"Exactly," Samantha said. "The more information we have, the better."

They carried the books to a small, round table. It was tucked in a quiet corner that smelled musty.

"Check each book's Table of Contents first," Ryan said, grabbing one and opening it. It was called *Fairmont from the Beginning*. There were twelve chapters in total. The first was about the town's founding in 1688. The second was about Fairmont during the American Revolution. The third was about Fairmont *after* the Revolution. None of the chapters sounded like they'd have any information about an old house.

"This is just basic history," Ryan said, setting

Fairmont from the Beginning on the floor. Then he grabbed the next book off the pile.

They all continued searching quietly for the next few minutes. Then Samantha said, "I think I've got something!"

"Shhhh!" they heard Ms. K say from upstairs.

"Sorry, sorry!" Samantha replied. Then, in almost a whisper, "Look!"

The book she had was called *All Around the Town of Fairmount.* She was pointing to an entry in the Table of Contents. Josh and Ryan came around to see what it was—

Chapter 9: Fairmont's Oldest Houses

Samantha flipped through the pages until she got there. The first house in the chapter was called "The Hanson Manor." It was built in 1845 and burned down in 1911. There was an old black-

and-white photo of it. It had three stories and was painted white.

"Well, that's not it," Ryan said.

"Definitely not," Josh said. "See here? It says, 'The train station in the center of town was built where the Hanson Manor once stood.'"

"Okay, so that's one down," Samantha said. Then she went to the next page.

There were nineteen houses mentioned in the chapter. All had pictures. And none looked like the one at the edge of the woods.

"How can that be?" Samantha said after they got to the end. "How can *that* house not be mentioned here? I'm sure we didn't miss it."

Ryan sat down and pulled the book over. Then he started flipping each page very slowly.

"We already did that, dude," Josh reminded him.

"I know. But I'm wondering if maybe—"

He stopped suddenly, and his face became

very pale.

"Oh wow . . ." he said quietly. "I can't believe it."

"What?" Samantha asked. "What's the big deal?"

Ryan turned the book around so they could see it right-side up. Then Ryan pointed to the bottom corner of one page.

"See that?"

"Yeah, 177," Josh said. "That's the page number. Big deal."

Ryan pointed to the other side. "And there?"

"178," Josh replied. "Why are you showing us—"

"Just wait," Ryan said. He flipped another page, then pointed at the bottom corner again. "*Now* look."

"It's 179! So what?" Josh replied, shrugging his shoulders. "I don't know wh—oh, wait a sec . . ."

He looked at the number again. Then he leaned down close to make sure he wasn't imagining it.

"Whoa—it's *not* 179."

"Nope," Ryan said. "It's 183. Pages are missing. And see here?" He pointed to the crease between 177 and 183. There were little ragged edges of paper in it. "That's where they were torn out."

"Wow."

"A-ha!" Samantha said suddenly. "What about the index?"

Ryan flipped right to it. "Great idea. At the very least, we might get the name of the hou—"

He stopped again. Disbelief flooded into him. Into all three of them.

Some index entries had been carefully cut out.

Ryan put the book down and grabbed another. This time he went straight to the index.

More entries had been cut away. And more pages were missing. Same with every other book that had any information on Fairmont's houses.

"What the heck is going *on* here?" Samantha whispered.

Ryan shook his head. "I have no idea. But whatever it is, it probably isn't good."

"So then what do we do now?"

No one said anything for a long moment. Then Josh smiled.

"I think I have an idea . . ."

A half hour later, they were standing on the sidewalk in front of a small house. There were many other houses on the same street. But this was the only one with a sign in front of it—

FAIRMONT HISTORICAL SOCIETY

"Remember Mr. Claude?" Josh asked them. "From a few years ago?"

Samantha was nodding. "He came to our class to talk about the town."

"He's the town historian," Ryan added.

"That's right."

"He showed us all sorts of cool stuff,"

Samantha said. "Like a musket from the Civil War. And some bottles from the 1870s."

"Yeah, and he told us we could come here if we wanted to learn more."

"And you have?" Ryan asked Josh. "Seriously?"

Josh smacked him on the back of the head. "Thanks for sounding so surprised," he said.

"I am," Ryan replied. "But I have to admit, this was a really good idea."

"They *have* to have some information about the house here," Samantha said.

Josh nodded. "I would think so. Let's check it out."

A little silver bell jingled as they opened the door. The air smelled dry and dusty. There were display cases everywhere. Framed pictures lined the walls. In one of the cases was a pair of old gloves. Next to it was a ring of rusty keys. On the wall behind the case was a black-and-white picture of a soldier. Next to that was the soldier's actual uniform. It hung on a mannequin with no head.

On the other side of the room was a very long case. Behind it was a doorway with a curtain hanging in it. A man swept back the curtain and stepped out. He was so big that he looked like a ball filled with too much air. He almost didn't fit through the doorway.

"Can I help you?" Mr. Claude asked. He had silver hair and glasses. His voice was rough, as if his throat was filled with rocks. And he wasn't smiling at the moment. He didn't sound too happy, either.

"We're just looking around," Josh replied.

"Well, don't touch anything," Mr. Claude said. "There's a lot of valuable stuff in here." Then he disappeared back behind the curtain.

"Well, isn't he just warm and fuzzy?" Ryan

commented under his breath.

They went through the first room and didn't see anything helpful. There was another room next to it. There were four more mannequins, all with ladies' dresses. There was also some jewelry in a small case, and a few hats hanging on the wall. All very interesting—but nothing to do with the house in the woods.

"Hey, check that out," Ryan said. He was pointing to another doorway. Inside was a staircase that looked very old. And on the wall was a sign that read **TOWN ARCHIVES UPSTAIRS.**

Ryan turned to Josh. "Archives are records that people keep for—"

"I know what archives are, snotface," Josh said. "Or are you just looking for another slap to the head?"

Ryan put his hands up. "Just making sure."

It was like the school's library, but so much more. There were shelves and shelves of books, of course. There were also piles of magazines and boxes of newspapers. Most of the newspapers were copies of *The Fairmont Herald*. The earliest, they saw, were from the 1870s. They also found folders with all sorts of legal papers from the town. There were birth and death certificates. There were sales receipts. And one had a collection of pet licenses.

Checking out the shelves, Samantha said, "Hey, here are some local books, like the ones we saw at school!"

Josh and Ryan almost tripped over each other getting over there.

"Where's that one we found?" Ryan asked. "*All Around the Town of Fairmount?*"

Samantha looked at every title. "It's not here."

"Okay," Ryan went on. "What about *What to See in Fairmont?*"

She looked again. "Nope."

Josh leaned over her and scanned all the books very closely.

"Whoa . . . you know what?" he said. "*None* of them are here."

"He's right," Samantha said. "They're not here. Any of them . . ."

"Which books?" Ryan asked. He took off his glasses and squinted. "You guys know I can't see from far away, and you're both standing in front of me! Which books are you talking ab—"

"The ones with the missing pages!" Samantha told him. "And with stuff cut out of the indexes!"

Ryan's eyes widened. "What! *NONE* of them?"

"Every book that had information about that house," Samantha said, "is missing from this collection."

"But every book that *doesn't* have information

about the house," Josh said, "*is* here."

"Okay, then the newspapers," Ryan said. "Let's go through those!"

They started toward the boxes. "But which ones?" Samantha asked. "There are tons of them!"

"Between 1896 and 1904," Ryan replied.

"Why then?"

"Because of the houses that *were* in the books," Ryan said. "The one before the torn-out pages was built in 1896. And the first one after the torn-out pages was built in 1904."

They lifted each newspaper out of its box very carefully. They were so old that each page had to be turned very slowly. Worst of all, after nearly two hours no one had found anything about the old house.

"But this is interesting," Samantha said. "About six weeks' worth of issues are missing from this box." She held it up to show the "1901" written on the side. "From September to early

October."

Ryan, who had been sitting on the floor, crawled over to her.

"Let me see something . . ."

He began reading through the August issues.

"What are you looking for now?"

"I'm not sure," Ryan said. "Maybe there will be—"

"Can I help you kids?" someone asked. They recognized Mr. Claude's rough voice right away. They had been so busy with the newspapers they didn't hear him come up the stairs.

"Yes, I could use some help," Ryan replied. Josh and Samantha looked at each other in confusion. *What is Ryan doing???*

"I'm writing a report on president Theodore Roosevelt," Ryan went on. "In 1901, he was William McKinley's vice president. Then McKinley was shot and killed. That's how

Roosevelt became president."

"That's right." Mr. Claude seemed mildly impressed.

"President McKinley died in September. I was hoping to get some information about it in these newspapers. But——" Ryan said as he held up the box, "all the issues from that month are missing. And a few from October, too."

Mr. Claude didn't say anything at first. He only stared at Ryan in a weird way. It was like he was studying him or something.

Then he nodded. "They're down in my office," he said. "Let me get them for you."

"Thank you," Ryan replied with a smile.

Mr. Claude returned about ten minutes later with the missing issues. They were not in a cardboard box like all the others. Instead, they were kept in a box made of very hard plastic. And the lid had a lock on it.

Mr. Claude opened the lock with a key he kept in his pocket. "These are very delicate," he said as he handed them to Ryan. "So please be careful."

"I will, I promise."

They waited until he left again. Then they started with the issue on top of the pile. It was from the first week in September. The headline on the front page read **OUR PRESIDENT HAS BEEN SHOT**. There was also an article about the kidnapping of a woman named Ms. Stone. Another was about something in China called the "Boxer Rebellion." But most were about stuff happening around town.

When Ryan turned to page eleven, Samantha let out a gasp. Toward the bottom was a headline in small letters—

<u>NEW HOUSE BUILT ON SITE OF</u>
<u>CONOVER FARM</u>

Just beneath this was a black-and-white picture of the house. It was a little blurry and kind of grainy. But still . . .

"Whoa," Josh whispered. "That's it."
Ryan started reading the article. "A new house is being built where the old Conover farm used to be. The Conover family owned the land for three generations. But after the death of Harold Conover, the land went up for sale. It was then purchased by a Ms. Anna Young last month. Ms. Young moved down to Fairmont from Danvers, Massachusetts, where she had been—"

A big, beefy hand reached in and snatched the paper away. The three of them looked up in surprise. Mr. Claude stood over them looking as mad as a rattlesnake.

"That is *not* why you said you needed these!" he growled.

"I'm sorry," Ryan said, "but we just—"

Mr. Claude pointed toward the staircase. "Out, all of you!"

"Can't we just look at one th—"

"Do I need to call your parents?"

Samantha shook her head quickly. "Uh no, no need to do that. Come on, you guys . . ." She started pushing Josh and Ryan to the steps.

Once they were outside, Mr. Claude slammed the door behind them.

"He was more scared than anything else," Samantha said as they walked back.

Ryan nodded. "That's what I thought, too."

"At least we have a name now," Samantha

said. "Anna Young."

"Well, we can't ask anyone around here about her," Ryan replied. "That'll just get us into more trouble. Maybe we should go on Google and—"

"No," Josh said, cutting him off. He had also stopped walking. "I'm tired of researching this. Like we're doing homework or something."

Ryan looked confused. "Then what do you suggest we do? Do you think—"

The words suddenly died in his mouth. And the expression on his face changed. He no longer looked confused. Now he looked like all the adults they'd been talking about—both scared and angry.

"Josh," Samantha cut in. "*No.*"

But Josh was nodding slowly. He had a big smile now. And he didn't really seem like he was listening anymore. They both knew what this meant—he had made up his mind.

"Oh yes," he said. "It's time to find out what

the big secret is. And there's only one way to do that." Then he looked to Samantha and Ryan and asked, "Who's with me?"

Neither of them answered.

The next day, Josh, Ryan, and Samantha
were standing along the edge of the woods again.
It was a Saturday, so no school. The house was
still a good distance away. Maybe the length of a
football field.

Josh took a deep breath. He was smiling
again, the other two noticed. Just like yesterday.

"Right," he said. "Let's do it!"

He started walking. Samantha and Ryan
trailed close behind.

"Josh," Ryan said. "You really don't need to
go in there. We've got a *name* now!"

"And you found . . . ?"

Ryan's shoulders slumped. "Nothing."

Josh laughed. "See? I told you. *We have to go inside.*"

They were about halfway there now.

"But we don't," Samantha said. "Don't you see that? It's not *that* important."

"It is to me," Josh replied.

When they got within a few feet, they stopped. The house was unbelievably huge up close. It was like looking up the side of a cliff.

"Josh," Samantha said. "How much of this is about your dad? About being mad at him? About getting even with him?"

"It's a little bit about that," Josh said. "But it's also because I'm curious. And because this is cool." His smile came back. "I mean, come on. Isn't this just *so* cool?"

"It is," Ryan said. "But it's also . . . I don't know. There's just something *wrong* about this place."

"No one wants to talk about it," Samantha

added. "And no one wants anyone else going near it. That scares me."

"It scares me, too," Josh admitted. Then he straightened himself. "But not enough to stop me from checking it out."

Ryan rolled his eyes. "Josh, you really shouldn't."

"He's right," Samantha said. "Don't go in there, please. If you really want to know about it, we'll figure something out."

But Josh shook his head.

"No. I'm doing this. And if you guys don't want to join, fine. Stay here."

Samantha grabbed him by the arm. "Are you crazy? You can't do it alone! What if something happens to you?"

"Then come with me."

No one said anything for a long moment. A strong wind breathed over the house. Then a low moan rose from somewhere. It was the sound of great age, and of great pain. It was also the scariest sound any of them had ever heard.

"Josh . . ." Samantha begged one more time.

"I'm going," he said. "Are you?"

She closed her eyes and sighed. "Fine."

Josh turned to Ryan. "You?"

"No way," he said.

"All right, then you're our lookout man."

"Woo-hoo," Ryan said without meaning it. "Aren't I the lucky one . . ."

Josh turned back to the house. He looked up at the sheer massiveness of it. It suddenly seemed like a living thing. A living thing that was looking back down at him. "Okay," he said. "Here we go . . ."

Josh and Samantha put their feet on the first step. The moment they did, the mysterious figure reappeared in the upstairs window.

Then it vanished again.

Every sense in Josh's body was on high
alert. He felt like he was seeing everything, hearing
everything, smelling everything. *This is crazy,* he
thought over and over. *But I'm still doing it.*

He and Samantha went up the steps slowly.
The boards creaked beneath them. Boards that
were old and dry. And felt like they hadn't been
used in a very long time.

They got to the front porch and stopped to
look around. There was plenty of room for a table
and some chairs or whatever. Josh had seen front
porches like this before. They were usually happy
places. People sat out on warm summer nights.
They talked and laughed and waved to others

walking by. This one wasn't anything like that. There were no tables or chairs. There was nothing. Nothing but creaky wood and cobwebs spun into the corners.

They went to the front door. It was as timeworn as everything else. But they could see that it had been nice once. The knob was beautifully designed. It looked to be made of some goldish metal. Brass, maybe. There was no shine to it anymore, though. In the top half of the door was a window. It also had a beautiful design. *That's called an etching,* Josh thought. *Cut right into the glass.* There were all sorts of dips and swirls and flowery-looking things. And there was so much design work that they couldn't really see through to the other side.

He took a deep breath. Then he wrapped his hand around the knob. At first it didn't feel like it was going to turn. *It's locked?!* he wondered in surprise. He never even considered this possibility.

The house was over a hundred years old, after all. *And where in the world would the key be anyway?* Then the knob finally did turn, although not easily. It sounded like there was dirt or sand inside of it.

The door itself also seemed to be stuck. It held there for a moment, refusing to move. Then Josh put his knee on the bottom half and pushed. It gave way with a horrible grinding sound. It was as if the door was angry at being opened.

They let it drift back and clunk against the wall. The first thing they noticed then was the smell. There was more dustiness and mustiness. But there was also something underneath that. Something much deeper. It was the scent of *age*. Of a great amount of time having passed.

In front of them now was a long hallway. There was a staircase on the left, going up. On the right, the hall led toward some other doors. There was no furniture in here. No decoration, either, like pictures hanging in frames. Just like the front porch, there was nothing. Chunks of plaster had broken off the walls and ceiling over the years. They now lay scattered all over the floor.

Josh stepped in first, Samantha right behind him. Their footsteps seemed very loud. They moved ahead carefully, studying everything.

"I'm not going up those stairs," Samantha said in a low voice.

"I'm not either," Josh replied. "At least not yet."

They kept walking until they came to the first door. It was on the right, and it was fully closed.

Josh opened it gently. The hinges squealed as it floated back. Then he and Samantha saw what was behind it.

It was a living room—a very large one. There were rows of tall windows on either side. Some had shades, the kind that needed to be pulled down. The shades were ripped and curled.

They hung crookedly from their rollers. There were also curtains. Once white, they were now a very light brown. And there were more holes in the walls and ceiling, more chunks of plaster scattered around. The walls were light blue, the ceiling white.

In the center of the room was a giant rug. A long couch was on one side of it. A rocking chair was on the other side. A little table stood next to the chair. All of this furniture was *covered* in dust. So much, in fact, that it was hard to tell what color any of it was.

At the other end of the room was a huge fireplace. The kind that was so big you could almost stand in it. And above that was an equally gigantic mirror inside a gold frame. It was tilted forward a little bit, like a big eye staring at them. Josh and Samantha could see themselves standing there.

They stepped inside. More creaks from the

floorboards. More dust being stirred up, probably for the first time in decades.

"This really is a creepy place," Josh said.

"Tell me about it," Samantha replied. She went over to the rocking chair and the little table. Then she stopped and sniffed the air.

"Do you smell that?" she asked.

"Smell what?"

"It's like . . . smoke, maybe. Smoke and ashes. A *burnt* smell."

Josh glanced over at the windows on the right side. He could see Ryan out there, looking as worried as ever. "It's probably just the fireplace," he said.

"I don't think so. Look how clean it is," she told him as she pointed to it.

Fireplaces normally had clear signs of use. There would be smudges of gray inside from all the ash. And smudges of black from all the burning. But this one was spotlessly clean. There was also a set of small fire tools nearby, hanging in a little stand. There was a broom, a shovel, a long rod with a handle, and what looked like a pair of giant tweezers. They were as dusty as everything else. But otherwise they seemed like they'd never been used.

Samantha sniffed the air again.

"No, Josh," she said, "it's definitely something else. Like something's burning *now*."

But Josh wasn't paying any attention to her. He was waving in the window, trying to get Ryan's attention.

"How come he isn't waving back?" Josh wondered. "HEY, STUPID!!! OVER HERE!!!"

Ryan took no notice of him.

Josh tried opening the window, but it wouldn't budge. Then he knocked on the glass like it was a door. Still no reaction from Ryan.

"It's like he can't hear at all," he said.

Then his sneaker kicked something on the

floor. It made a bright, jingly sound.

"Uh-oh," he said as he looked down.

"What's wrong?"

"Be careful," he told her, pointing to where several large pieces of broken glass lay.

Samantha came over to take a closer look. "That's the same kind of glass in all these windows," she said.

"Yeah, definitely."

"But . . . none of the windows are broken."

Josh looked around the room and saw that she was right. Even the window right above the broken glass was in good shape. Not so much as a crack.

Josh pointed again. "Then where did this come from?"

"I don't know," Samantha replied, still looking at it. "But I think we should get out of—"

When she stopped talking, Josh turned to her. "Sam? What's wrong?"

Her eyes had widened until they were bulging. And her mouth was hanging open again.

"My God, *look*—"

Josh followed the direction of her finger. Then his eyes popped open, too. There were spots of some kind of liquid on the floor—and they were bright red.

"Is that . . . what I think it is?" he asked.

"It sure looks like it."

They both crouched down to take a closer look. Samantha reached out a finger to touch it. Then she changed her mind and pulled it back.

"That's blood," Josh said. "I know it when I see it."

"Yeah, me too. And check that out—"

She pointed again to show him that the spots continued in a line. The line went along the wall, then turned at the corner. From there it went to the doorway and back out to the hall.

Samantha looked at Josh directly. Her eyes

were wild with fear and confusion. "It isn't just blood. It's *fresh* blood," she said.

"Yeah," Josh replied. "I see that." His voice was a little shaky now.

"How is that possible?"

"I have no idea. But that's not even the creepiest part. You know what is?"

"The fact that it wasn't here when we first came in?"

Josh nodded. "Yeah. I'm sure of it. I looked over *everything* when we walked in here."

"Me too. There's no way I would've missed it."

"Okay, then you know what?" They both stood back up.

"It's time to get the heck out of here?"

"Yeah," he told her. "Let's go."

They grabbed each other's hand and made for the door. In the hallway, they saw the blood trail continue. It went back the way they came when they first walked in. Then it turned at the staircase. Some of the blood spots crossed through the footsteps they made in the dust.

"See?" Josh said. "I'm sure we would've noticed that when we came in."

"*So* creepy," Samantha replied. They hurried toward the door that led outside. "I'm sorry I ever came in here."

"Yeah, me too."

"It was your idea, Josh. You just *had* to know the big secret here."

"I'm sorry about that," he told her. "But I'm over it now, and I promise never to come back here to—"

They had reached the door, and Josh pulled it open. Then it felt like everything in the world came to a stop.

"Wha . . ." Samantha began. "What is this?"

Josh didn't say anything back. He just stood there and stared.

The outside had *disappeared*. There was no Ryan anymore. No empty field in front of the house. No forest in the distance. No blue sky. No clouds.

Instead, there was another room.

They both stood there for awhile. Maybe half a minute. But it felt like forever.

Finally, Josh said, "Sam, what's going on here?"

Samantha shook her head. "I have no idea."

This "new" room was like the other one in certain ways. There was some old furniture, a big rug, and a few windows. But the walls were pale green rather than light blue. And there was no fireplace or mirror. There also weren't any blood spots on the floor.

Samantha put one foot inside very carefully. "The floor's solid," she said. "It's real."

Josh did the same. Then he said, "How?

How is this possible?" He sounded angry now. But Samantha had known him all her life. Underneath that anger was pure fear. It was like a pot of water on a stove. And it was getting very close to boiling over.

Samantha stepped all the way in. She went to an old chair and touched it. There was a lamp standing next to it. It was almost as tall as Samantha was. She ran her fingers over that, too.

Josh had come inside by this time. He walked over to one of the windows. Its shade was about halfway down, just like all the others. He gave the shade a quick jerk along the bottom, then let go. It rolled up to the top, making lots of noise along the way. Then he looked outside.

"No way . . ." he said.

Samantha turned and saw it, too. Her hand went to her mouth.

"Josh!"

"I know."

Even though the window was dirty, they could see through it with no trouble. The field was there. So were the trees, and the sky, and the clouds. The problem was—

"It's wrong," Josh said. "This is the *back* of the house."

Samantha nodded. "Yeah."

"But the back is *that way*!" He pointed in an entirely different direction.

"I know, I know!"

He tried to open the window, but it was frozen in place. Just like the window in the other room.

Josh looked outside for another long moment, shaking his head.

"That's it. We're getting out of here right now."

"What do you mean?"

"I mean this . . ."

He walked over to the lamp next to the

chair. Then he grabbed it and turned it sideways. He looked like a knight holding a lance.

"Here we go," he said.

He aimed carefully and ran forward. The lamp hit the window dead center, and the glass exploded into a million pieces. Then Josh let the lamp go, and it flew through the hole to the other side. Fresh air rushed in. It smelled good, sweet.

"Okay," he said, reaching for Samantha's hand. "Let's get out of—oh my God, NO!"

Everything outside changed. It was like in a movie, where one scene faded into another. The field, the trees, the blue sky—it all disappeared. And in its place . . .

"Another room," Samantha said. She didn't sound scared or upset or even angry. She spoke the words flatly, almost like a computer. "What . . . what are we going to do now?"

Josh thought for a moment.

"I'll tell you what we're gonna do," he replied.

Then he took out his phone.

Ryan didn't just feel nervous anymore. He felt sick. He felt like he might even throw up. That's what happened when things got really crazy in his life.

Where ARE they? he kept wondering. It hadn't been that long since they went inside. Maybe fifteen minutes at the most. But he didn't see them anywhere. Josh said he'd wave from one of the windows, to let him know they were okay. That hadn't happened yet. Ryan didn't even see them walking by any of the windows. So now his imagination was working like a machine in high gear. Did one of them get hurt? Did they *both* get hurt? Was the house really haunted? Did some ghost or vampire get them?

I can't take it any more, he thought, and reached for his phone. The moment he did, it rang.

He saw Josh's name on the screen and answered immediately. But he didn't get very far.

"*There* you are! Why haven't—"

"Just shut up and listen to me," Josh said. Then he told Ryan everything that had happened up to that point. The more Josh talked, the sicker Ryan felt.

"I . . . I can't believe it," Ryan said. His stomach was turning over like clothes in a washing machine.

"Well, believe it."

"I *told* you not to go in there."

"Yeah, I already got that from Sam. I don't need it from you, too. What I really need you to do is go get help."

"From who? Your parents?"

"No."

"The police?"

"No, not—"

"Do you want me to call—"

"*RY*!!!"

Ryan actually jumped a little.

"Sorry, sorry." He was doing this weird little thing now where he flapped one hand in the air. It looked like he was trying to shake water off it or something. This was a sign that he was *really* starting to come apart.

"Who, then?"

"Mr. Claude."

"What?! He's not going to—"

"He knows more than he's letting on," Josh said. "I can tell. I've seen that look before. And think about it—he's the town historian. He's got to know *something*."

Ryan started nodding. Slowly at first, then faster.

"Yeah, that's a good idea."

"Then get moving," Josh said. "And make it quick, okay?"

"Okay."

He ran into the woods and reached the fence. By the time he got under it and back to his bike, he was crying.

When Ryan got to the Fairmont Historical Society, he dropped his bike on the lawn and kept running. It took Mr. Claude a few minutes to answer the door

"Oh, it's you again," he said. He was clearly unhappy at being disturbed. "What do you wa—"

"We need help!" Ryan said, panting. "Please!"

"I cannot help you with anything concerning that old house," Mr. Claude replied. "And you are not to ask about it aga—"

"They went inside!" Ryan said. "And now they're trapped!"

Mr. Claude's eyes widened behind his

glasses.

"*Who* went inside? Your other two friends?"

Ryan nodded. "Yes," he said. Then he repeated everything that had happened so far.

"E-*gads*!" came Mr. Claude's shocked reply. He looked around the neighborhood to make sure no one was watching them. Then he waved Ryan inside. "Okay . . . come in, come in!"

He shut the door and told Ryan to wait. Then he disappeared into his back room for a moment. Ryan could hear the sounds of things being moved around—papers, boxes, empty soda cans. Then Mr. Claude returned with more of the old newspapers. They were the same ones he'd snatched out of Ryan's hands the other day.

He set them on the counter. "You and your friends should not be going anywhere near that house," he said. He sounded both angry *and* scared now.

"I told Josh that," Ryan said.

"He is the tall one?" Mr. Claude asked as he searched through each issue. "With all the hair on top?"

Ryan nodded. "Yes."

"And the girl?"

"Samantha. She didn't want to go in, either. But she didn't want Josh to do it alone."

Mr. Claude laughed a little. But it wasn't a *funny* laugh. In fact, there wasn't anything funny about it at all.

"Yes, well, sometimes being a friend comes at a great price," he said.

Ryan rolled his eyes. "Tell me about it."

Mr. Claude kept thumbing through the newspapers. "Where is it?" he mumbled to himself over and over. Then he said, "Ah!" and set one down on top of the others. Ryan saw the date at the top of the front page—October 4, 1901.

Mr. Claude began paging through it quickly. He didn't seem as worried about the age of the paper as the last time Ryan was there.

"Look here," he said, pointing to a headline on page seven—

ANNA YOUNG HOUSE BURNS TO THE GROUND

At about 3:00 a.m. last night, firemen were called to the house built just two months ago by Ms. Anna Young, a new resident in Fairmont. They raced heroically to the scene and found the house engulfed in flames. But due to its distant location on the former Conover property, they were unable to put it out before it burned to the ground. Hank Colson, Fairmont's Fire Chief, said the cause of the blaze may have been a towel accidentally left on a stove. Ms. Young, however, could not be reached for comment. Town officials believe she has since left the area and returned to her hometown of Danvers, Massachusetts.

Ryan looked up at Mr. Claude.

"How can this be right?" he asked. "The house didn't burn down! It's still there! I saw it myself!"

Mr. Claude nodded. "I know. It burned down, then it reappeared the very next day."

"WHAT???"

"That's why no one is supposed to go near it. Everyone's afraid of it."

Ryan was shaking his head. "But that's impossible! It can't just *come back*!"

"Can't it?" Mr. Claude pointed to a spot at the bottom of the article. "See that?"

Ryan looked at the word just under Mr. Claude's chubby finger—*Danvers*.

"Yeah, so? It's where she lived before she came here. So what?"

"Does it sound familiar at all?"

Ryan scanned through his memory but came up with nothing.

"Not really," he replied.

"It's one of the most famous towns in the entire United States, young man."

Ryan's eyebrows went up in disbelief. "Then why haven't I heard of it?"

"Oh, you have," Mr. Claude said. "But you probably know it much better by its *original* name— Salem Village."

It took Ryan only a millisecond to make the connection. Then all the color seemed to drain out of his face.

"You mean 'Salem' as in the place where . . . where . . ."

Mr. Claude nodded. "Yeah—where the Salem Witch Trials took place."

"Oh my God . . ." Josh said. He was on the verge of a total breakdown. "A witch . . . a *witch*!" He sat on the floor and covered his face with his hands.

Samantha was standing next to him, holding her phone out. "Are you sure, Ryan?"

"As sure as we can be," came Ryan's voice through the little speaker.

"It all fits," Mr. Claude added in the background. "She would have left Danvers to escape persecution."

"That's when someone gets into trouble for their beliefs," Ryan said.

"I know what it means, Ryan," Samantha

replied. "But were witches really still being persecuted in the early 1900s?"

"Sure," Mr. Claude said. "There are still places in the world where they're hunted *today*."

"You're kidding."

"Not at all. Have you heard of the terrorist group called ISIS?" he asked.

"Sure," Samantha said. "I heard about them on the news."

"In June of 2015, they killed people whom they believed to be using magic to treat sickness."

"That's insane," she said.

"Absolutely," Mr. Claude agreed.

Josh was shaking his head as he fought back tears. "My parents are going to kill me," he kept saying. "They're going to *kill* me!"

Since none of this was helpful, Samantha decided to ignore him.

"So then why would she go *back* to Danvers after the house burned down?" she asked.

"It doesn't make any sense," Ryan said.

Samantha thought about all the rooms they'd been in since Ryan left. She counted a total of forty-two. Some were living rooms. Others were bedrooms. Two were kitchens. Most had no furniture or decoration of any kind. But a few had everything. One of the living rooms had nice lamps and framed pictures and piles of magazines. And one of the bedrooms had a makeup table and bottles of perfume and a book on the nightstand. (The book was Mark Twain's classic *Adventures of Huckleberry Finn*. She'd read it in school the year before. The fact that a witch had also read it freaked her out a little bit.)

Samantha realized how the whole room-changing thing worked. Once they walked into a room, the one behind them changed. The new one could be anything—sitting room, bedroom, whatever. Some had ten windows, others had only two or three. Some were nice, others were empty and dusty. So there was no pattern to what kind of room would appear behind them.

She did, however, notice a pattern in something else.

"Ryan," she said, "let me call you and Mr. Claude right back."

"Um, okay . . ." Ryan replied. "What's going on?"

"Nothing, just . . . I'll call you right back."

She grabbed Josh's hand and lifted him to his feet. His eyes were red and puffy.

"What are you doing?" he asked.

"Follow me," she said. "You'll see."

They went through nine different rooms until they found the one Samantha wanted. There was a small table with a black bowl. The bowl had ashy smudges inside. There were also some glass bottles on a little shelf. Each one was a different color—dark blue, dark red, yellow, green—but you could still see through them. Some had powder inside. Others had liquid. A big iron pot hung from a chain. And there were a few large candles set on tall stands. Like the bottles, the candles were many different colors.

"Why did you want to come back here?" Josh asked.

"I have a hunch . . ." Samantha said. She went to a shelf that had some very old books. Each one was about witchcraft. There was also something rolled up next to them. It looked like a small, black towel. Samantha took it down and unrolled it.

"Just what I thought," she said. Then she showed it to Josh. There was a shape stitched into the fabric. It was a five-pointed star inside a circle.

His eyes flew open, and he pointed with a shaking finger.

"That's the sign of the devil!" he said.

Samantha shook her head. "Josh . . ."

"It's . . . it's a *pentagram*!"

"That's right, a pentagram. But it has nothing to do with the devil."

"Of course it does! Everyone knows that!"

"Josh, the pentagram has been mostly used as a religious symbol. Christians have used it, and so have Jews. But it's also used by those who practice magic—usually *white* magic."

Josh looked puzzled. "White magic? What's that?"

"It's a type of magic used to *help* people. Like when someone gets sick. Or if someone travels and wants protection." She pointed to the multicolored candles. "See those? A white witch would use them in spells for different reasons. A red candle helps keep a person healthy. A blue candle can help someone sleep better. A green candle helps with growth."

"Seriously?"

"Seriously."

"I thought there was only black magic," Josh admitted.

"That's what most people think."

"So how do you know all this?"

"I've always been kind of interested in witchcraft," Samantha told him. "I've done a little reading on it. I'm not, like, an expert. But I think it's kind of neat."

"Okay," Josh said, "then tell me this. White magic is supposed to be only used for good, right?"

"Yes."

"Then why are we trapped in here? The woman who lived here obviously used some kind of a spell, didn't she? To make the house appear again after it was burned down?"

Samantha nodded. "There's no other way to explain it."

"So why bother doing that if she just went

back to her old town in Massachusetts anyway?"

Samantha took her phone out of her pocket. "I'm going to see about that right now. But I think I already know."

"Huh? I don't understand."

"Josh," she said, "I don't think Anna Young ever made it back to Massachusetts."

"This is a crazy idea," Ryan told Mr. Claude. "Josh's dad isn't the nicest man in the world. He's not going to be real happy."

"I'm sure he won't," was all Mr. Claude said back. "But I need to know the truth."

He pulled his car to the curb and parked it. Then he and Ryan got out. They went to the front door and rang the bell. Mr. Harper was there a moment later. He was dressed in cotton pants and a button-down shirt. And every hair was combed perfectly. *This is Saturday,* Ryan thought. *Doesn't he own even one pair of jeans?*

"Alan Claude? What can I do for—and Ryan? What's this all about?"

"Can we speak with you for a moment?" Mr.

Claude asked.

Mr. Harper didn't answer him right away. Ryan got the feeling there was something about Mr. Claude that Mr. Harper didn't like.

"Well . . . sure," he said finally. Then he led them into the living room. Once they were all seated, he said, "Ryan, where's Josh? I thought he was with you today."

"He was," Ryan replied. "But . . ."

Mr. Harper immediately looked suspicious. "But what?" There was a moment of uneasy silence. Then he said, "This better not have anything to do with that old house."

"It does," Mr. Claude said. "It has to do with the house. And the woman who lived there. Ms. Anna Young."

Ryan noticed Mr. Harper twitch a little when he heard Anna Young's name. *He knows something—and he's hiding it.*

"I ordered Josh not to go anywhere near that

place!" Mr. Harper said angrily.

"Well, he did," Mr. Claude told him. "He and their other friend, Samantha."

"Then the moment he gets home, he's—"

"Now they're trapped inside!" Ryan added.

Mr. Harper's eyes lit up with rage. "*WHAT*?!" he snarled.

"That's right," Ryan said as his heart pounded with fear. Then he told Mr. Harper about the rooms changing. And about the blood spots on the floor. And the things Anna Young had used in her witchcraft.

"This is *your* fault, isn't it?" Mr. Harper said to Mr. Claude. "You made them do this! You—"

"I had nothing to do with it, sir!" Mr. Claude replied. "And I think we both know whose fault this *really* is, don't we?"

Mr. Harper looked as if he'd been slapped. "How dare you—"

"Tell us the truth," Mr. Claude said. "Tell us

what really happened that night back in 1901!"

Mr. Harper stood up and pointed toward the door. "I want you both to leave right now!" he roared.

"We're trying to help save your son!" Mr. Claude roared back.

"Please, Mr. Harper," Ryan pleaded. "Please!"

Mr. Harper took his cell phone out of his pocket. "If you don't leave this second, I will call the police!"

Mr. Claude pulled a letter from his pocket. The envelope was so old the paper had turned brown around the edges. The postmark by the stamp said December 1901.

"If you don't answer my question," Mr. Claude said, taking the letter out, "then I will make sure everyone in town knows about this."

He held it up to Mr. Harper. Ryan had already seen it. It was written by a man named

Charles Pelton. Mr. Claude told Ryan he had lived in Fairmont a long time ago. Then the Peltons moved away—right after the fire that destroyed Anna Young's house. The letter hinted at a cover-up for a crime. It mentioned someone named Harper.

Mr. Harper's body language changed as he read the letter. All the anger seemed to go out of him. His shoulders sagged, his eyes turned downward. He put the phone back in his pocket.

"Mr. Harper," Ryan said. "Did the townspeople start that fire?" Before Mr. Harper had the chance to answer, Ryan added, "And was Anna Young still inside when they did?"

Mr. Harper looked scared now. Like an animal that knows it has no place left to run.

He nodded. "Yes," he said very quietly.

"I always had a feeling that's what happened," Mr. Claude said. "But I could never be sure because no one would talk about it. And your great-grandfather, Mr. Harper? He was one of the people who did it. Am I right?" Josh's dad nodded.

"Okay, thank you," Mr. Claude said. Then he and Ryan turned and began walking out.

Just as they got to the door, however, Josh's dad said, "He wasn't the only one, y'know. Not by a long shot."

Ryan turned back. "What do you mean?"

Just a few minutes later, he was sorry he asked that question.

Samantha and Josh sat next to each other on the floor. They both had their backs against the wall. And they were both crying.

"I can't believe it," Samantha said, still holding the phone in her hand. She had hung up with Ryan less than five minutes earlier. "I can't believe my great-great-grandmother took part in a witch hunt! Ryan's great-grandmother, too!"

"And *two* of my great-great-grandparents," Josh said. "Not to mention my great-great-uncle Carl." He shook his head. "My dad always talked about him like he was the nicest guy ever."

"Plus all those other people," Samantha went on, wiping the tears off her face. Fresh

90

ones came streaming down within seconds. "Past relatives of so many people we know in town. Mrs. Howard, our history teacher. Mr. Clarke, our postman. And Officer Tim. He's our Chief of Police!"

"I know," Josh said. "It's . . . it's *embarrassing*. I always thought Fairmont was such a great place."

"So did I."

"But . . . Sam, they murdered Anna Young. We're all related to *murderers*."

Samantha was shaking her head. "I know," she said miserably. "I know."

"And now we're trapped in here forever," Josh went on. "In the house that they burned down while she was still in it. This is how she's getting her revenge!"

He cried even harder now—but Samantha suddenly stopped.

"Wait a minute . . ." she said. "Just wait . . . one . . . minute . . ."

"What?" Josh asked.

"She was able to make this house reappear after it was burned, right?"

"Yeah, so?"

"And when the rooms behind us disappear, new rooms appear in their place. She obviously did that, too. A spell of some kind."

"Yeah . . ."

"That's some pretty amazing magic, wouldn't you say? I mean, the thing with the rooms changing still works after more than a hundred years. Pretty powerful stuff, *right*?"

"Definitely."

"Then why didn't she just kill everyone? Everyone responsible for killing *her*, I mean. Why didn't she just put a curse on them or something?"

Josh shrugged. "I don't know."

Samantha looked at Josh directly. "Yes you do. Think about it."

He went into deep-thought mode for a few moments. Then he looked back at her and said, "Because she was a *white* witch?"

"That's right."

"And white witches don't hurt people."

"That's right."

"They only try to help them."

Samantha was nodding. "You got it."

"But she's hurting us *now*," Josh said. "By trapping us in here!"

Now Samantha shook her head the other way.

"No, Josh. I don't think that's it. I don't think hurting us is what Anna Young wants."

"It isn't?"

"No."

Samantha got up and held her hand out. Then she lifted Josh off the floor for the second time that day.

"Follow me," she said. "If I'm right, maybe

we can solve more than one problem at the same time."

They found their way back to the room that had the big fireplace with the mirror over it. Then Samantha led Josh to the broken glass under the window.

"The blood spots," she said, pointing.

"What about them?"

"They run off in that direction. To the corner, turn right, and go out the door."

"So?"

"Did you notice where they went next?"

"No. What does that matter?"

"More than you might think," she said.

They followed the trail out into the hall. Their footprints were still clearly visible in the dust from before. The footprints went to the front door of the house. But the blood spots went somewhere else . . .

"Up the stairs," Josh said. "I never saw that."

"Neither did I until a minute ago," Samantha told him. "We've been so freaked out about everything else."

Josh traced the path of the spots with his eyes.

"So, do we go up there?" he asked.

"If we ever want to get out of here," Samantha replied.

They went up the steps to the second floor. It was even dustier and creakier than the first. They had to use the lights on their phones because it was so dark. The spot-trail took them down another long hallway. Then it turned and went under a closed door.

Grabbing the doorknob, Samantha took a deep breath.

"I really hope I'm right about this," she said. Then she opened the door and let it fly back.

Inside was a small bedroom. It had all the normal things in it. There was a hairbrush on the dresser. A long mirror hung in a stand in one corner. And there was a small table with some paper on it. Next to the paper was a bottle of ink and a very old pen.

Sniffing the air, Samantha said, "That burning smell is very strong in here."

"More than in any other room," Josh replied.

Samantha pointed to the bed.

"The top blanket is missing," she said.

"So?"

"So, I'm not sure. Hang on . . ."

She went to the table and looked closely at the ink. Then she turned back to Josh.

"It's still wet," she said. She tapped the tip of the pen with her finger. A small black dot appeared there. "See?"

"Okay, so what does that mean?"

Samantha looked down at the blood spots again. They made a line that went to the foot of the bed. Then they turned and crossed the room. Finally, they made one last turn before going under another door.

"The closet," Samantha said in a whisper. "Oh no . . ."

She walked over there slowly. Josh followed her without saying a word.

She put her hand on the knob of the closet door.

She turned it.

The door opened.

And there, curled up in the missing blanket, was the skeleton of Anna Young. She was still holding a folded sheet of paper in one hand. Samantha gently took the paper from her. Unfolding it, she found just one sentence, in Anna's own handwriting—

Please bury my body so my soul can rest in peace.

Anna Young's funeral was held two days later. Everyone in Fairmont came to the service. Then her remains were placed in the town cemetery.

A short time later, Josh, Samantha, and Ryan went walking through the woods again.

"It's funny how the rooms all stopped changing after we found her," Josh said.

"I think it's because the spell was broken then," Ryan replied. "I'm sure she did it that way on purpose. If she wanted someone to bury her, they'd have to be able to get out of the house."

Josh nodded. "Exactly."

"Why do you think our cell phones

worked?" Samantha asked.

"I've been wondering about that, too," Ryan said.

"It's probably because there were no cell phones back in Anna Young's time," Josh guessed.

Ryan nodded. "I agree. She couldn't have known about them. So her spell wouldn't be able to stop them."

"We were really lucky there," Samantha said. "Can you imagine what would have happened otherwise?"

Josh trembled all over. "I don't even want to think about that."

Ryan sighed. "I still can't believe what they did to her."

"My mom told me that they all thought Anna was evil." Samantha shook her head. "That's what she heard from *her* grandmother."

"My dad showed me this letter," Josh said. "It was from my great-great-grandfather to some friend of his in Ohio. He said a witch had just moved to Fairmont. He thought she was going to turn everyone in town into animals. Then she was going to keep them on the Conover farm until she ate them."

"How can we be *related* to people like that?" Ryan asked.

"Because most people are scared of things they don't understand," Samantha said. "And because even grown-ups aren't perfect. It's easy to think they have all the answers. But the truth is they don't."

"You got that right," Josh replied. "My dad has really changed since all this happened. He's been nicer to me than ever."

"I can't believe he knew the whole time," Ryan said.

"They all did," Samantha added. "Even *my* parents knew. Although they hated keeping it secret. But just like those people back in 1901, they were too scared to do anything about it."

They reached the fence and went under. Then they headed up the path that led to the field. As soon as they got there, they stopped.

"Oh my God . . ." Samantha whispered. Josh and Ryan said nothing. They just stood there and stared.

The house that had once belonged to Anna Young was gone. Not even a trace of it remained. There was nothing but tall grass, bright sun, and a light wind from the north.

"She's finally at peace," Samantha said.

"I think you're right," Ryan agreed.

Josh was nodding. "Yeah, probably. But what about the rest of the town?"

None of them had an answer to that.

They began walking back.

Want to Keep Reading?

Turn the page for a sneak peek at
the next book in the series.

ISBN: 9781538383643

The door swung back and clunked against the wall. Then Delilah came in dragging the little couch. She was huffing and puffing. She brought the couch to the center of the room and put it down. It was light green with flowers all over it.

She sat on it to catch her breath. The pain in her arms was terrible. So was the pain in her back, her shoulders, her legs . . . *everything* seemed to hurt. But she was happy. It took forever to get the couch down the basement steps. *But it was worth it*, she thought. *Totally worth it.*

Delilah Bremmer was thirteen. She was very skinny, and she had long hair that was as black as hair could be. Her eyes were ocean blue like her mom's. She also had her mom's tan skin. Her mom had been born in Mexico. Delilah had gone there twice to visit family with her mom. Her dad went with them. Those were good times. The best, in fact.

Delilah thought about one of those trips to Mexico as she sat on the green couch. She remembered this restaurant they'd visited. The power kept going out because there was a big storm. The lights flickered every time thunder boomed. But the cook somehow made their food anyway. Her parents didn't care that it took so long, either. They were laughing until they could barely breathe. What a crazy, fun night that was.

Then she shoved these thoughts out of her mind. *Too busy right now*, she thought. *Way too busy.* And too busy to think about school, too. About how much she hated it these days. And how much trouble she'd been getting into lately. And how angry this made her mom . . .

Way too busy to think about it, she thought again.

She got up and went to the other couch in the room. It was a nice couch—but it wasn't the *right* one.

She leaned down to get her fingers under it. Then she dragged it out. When she came back, she put the new couch in its place. She stepped back and gave it a good looking-over. She smiled, and a warm feeling washed through her.

It's perfect, she told herself. *At last . . . everything is RIGHT.*

She lay on the new couch and tucked her hands behind her head. Then she looked at everything else in the room—the flat-screen TV, the cordless telephone, the PlayStation . . . It really was right, all of it. Because it was all four years old. *Exactly* four.

Delilah got the idea from a message someone sent her on AllMyFriends. At first it looked like just another junky, irritating ad. The person who sent it had no profile picture and no real name. Then she saw this at the top—

HOW WOULD YOU LIKE TO GO BACK TO THE BEST DAYS OF YOUR LIFE?

Below that was a link to an article. The article was about putting together a room from another time. It was called a "retro room." She looked up "retro" in a dictionary. It meant: "Having to do with an earlier time." The article said you needed to fill a room with things from that time. The more "time-correct" the things were, the better the room would be.

At the bottom of the article was the comments section. One guy from Canada said he made a retro room from 1966. That was his senior year in high school. A married couple from Arizona said they had a retro room from 1993. That was the year they met.

Then Delilah saw a comment that really caught her attention. The person's screen name was LonelyGirl99. She lived in Florida, and her parents were no longer married. LonelyGirl99 wanted to go back to the time when her mom and dad were still together. When they all lived in the same house. And they did things as a family. And there was no yelling. Or slamming doors. Or sadness.

Or sadness . . .

Those last two words shot through Delilah like an arrow. *I'd give anything to go back to the days when there was no sadness. Anything in the world.*

Her parents had split up last year. She begged them to get back together. But they wouldn't. She couldn't understand why. They had been so in love at one time. What had changed? *How* had it changed? And *why* did her parents have to be so stupid about everything? Couldn't they see what it was doing to her? Didn't they know how ripped-apart she felt? Didn't they *CARE*?

No, Delilah realized. *They don't.*

So she decided to make a retro room just like LonelyGirl99. A room from back when everything was perfect. And she'd visit it as much as possible. Even if her parents didn't like the idea—and they didn't. But that was too bad. She was going to do this.

Delilah had to look through old pictures her mom had taken with her phone. She'd cried a lot when she went through those pictures. But she had to do it. She made a list of the things that reminded her of those great days. Many of them weren't in the house anymore. Her dad had taken some when he moved out. Other things had been sold or thrown away.

Delilah went to yard sales. She went to the thrift store in town. And she found some things on eBay. Her grandma gave her the money she needed. Delilah called her "G-ma." G-ma was like her best friend. She seemed to know exactly how Delilah felt. She was perfectly okay with Delilah's idea for the room. She even helped her carry some things downstairs and set them up.

And now, more than a year later, it was done. Every single thing was the same as in the house four years ago. The chairs, the lamps, the pictures . . . everything. It was all "time-correct," like the article said.

Just one last thing, Delilah thought. *And I'll get that on the way home from school tomorrow.*

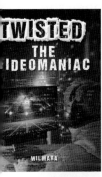
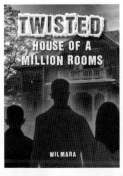

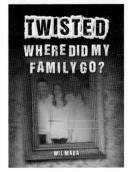
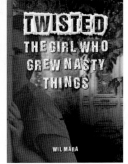

ABOUT THE AUTHOR

Wil Mara has been an author for over 30 years and has more than 200 books to his credit. His work for children includes more than 150 educational titles for the school and library markets, and he has also ghostwritten five of the popular Boxcar Children mysteries. His 2013 thriller *Frame 232* reached the #1 spot in its category on Amazon and won the Lime Award for Excellence in Fiction. He is also an associate member of the NJASL, and an executive member of the Board of Directors for the New Jersey Center for the Book, an affiliate of the U.S. Library of Congress. He lives with his family in New Jersey.